Praise for the Writing of Jan McCanless'

"In these days of stress we can all use a good laugh! This book is bound to make you smile and laugh. Jan's quirky sense of humor and outlook on life will do just that! So forget your troubles, kick your shoes off, sit back and enjoy this delightful read!" —Marie Norway, Author, singer, songwriter, radio and TV personality

"McCanless is a well-known, award-winning humorist yes, but her reflections are insightful and her humor is iconic, contemporary and inspirational. She has a knack for getting us all to laugh at ourselves as we agree with her timeless truths. My go-to read." —Sherry Rentschler, bestselling author of *Time and Blood*, Book 1, Evening Bower Series

"Jan McCanless writes with humor, and Southern flair that makes her mysteries even more fun to read."—Author Marni Graf, writer of the Nora Tierney and Truly Genova Manhattan series

"Jan McCanless has the uncanny ability to spin a yarn that is not only enjoyable, but, a good, easy read, perfect for a lazy day in front of a roaring fire, or a crashing wave at the ocean. I have spent a goodly number of hours at the beach, which I am sure is close to Beryl's Cove, immersed in her delightful stories." — Camille Jones, retired ESL Teacher

"My favorite author, yours too after reading one of her books!" — Robert G. Hyers, retired engineer, Scientific Atlanta

Empower

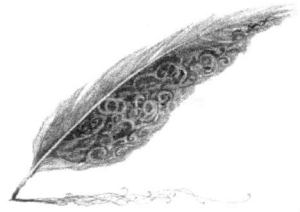

Publishing

Also by Jan McCanless

Beryl's Cove Stories
Murder at the Stateline Motel
Murder on the Rocks
Gold, Frankincense and Murrrder
Murder for the Profit
Who Killed theWeatherman
The Choir Loft Murders
All Aboard for Murder
The Haunted Chapel
Great Scott
The Case of the Doomed Diplomat
Beryl's Cove and the Elvis Man

Brother Jerome Series
The Opera House Murders
Murder in Midair
Murder on the Mississippi

Jimmie and Harlan Books
Murder at the Stateline Motel

Compilations
The Bizarre Brain Drippings of a Noted Sagittarian and More
Thoughts of Home
Laugh Out Loud Funny Stuff, Brain Drippings Book Two
Tire Patch Cookies are Good for the Soul
Wyatt Earp, GAP Pickles and Thoughts of Home – Winner of the
Mother Vine Award

Manual
The In$ and Out$ of Writing for Money

The Mysterious Beryl's Cove

By

Jan McCanless

Empower Publishing
Winston-Salem

Empower

Publishing

Empower Publishing
PO Box 26701
Winston-Salem, NC 27114

First Empower Publishing Books edition published September, 2022

Empower Publishing, Feather Pen and all production design are trademarks.

For information regarding bulk purchases of this book, digital purchase and special discounts, please contact the publisher at publish.empower.now@gmail.com

Cover design by Pan Morelli

Manufactured in the United States of America
ISBN 978-1-63066-546-3

To treasure hunters everywhere, may you find your own rainbow and pot of gold! and for mystery lover everywhere, I'm so glad you enjoy my "Happy Murders." They are all for you.

—Jan

Prologue

The hurricane churned up the Atlantic, causing 30-foot swells, as it made its way from the West African coast, fighting its way across the expanse of water.

Gaining strength with every wave, it was heading straight for the Bahamas. Every weather report gave new coordinates, and new evacuation notices were issued. It was a killer storm, on a par with Katrina and other massive, destructive storms. This one, however, was staying in the Atlantic, expected later in the week to hit the eastern coast of the United States.

The waves swelled and rolled, tossing seagoing ships around like toys. An oil tanker, from the Mideast, rolled so far over, two of her crew were washed overboard, unable to be rescued, they soon sank into the depths.

Every captain of every ship at sea, fought for control of his vessel, and every sick bay was soon at capacity of seasick sailors, retching their guts out.

On Nassau, weather spotters stood watch on the beach, watching as the waves intensified, and thrashed upon the sand, a look of worry on their faces. Unable to control mother nature at her worst, they could only watch, and hope their island took only a sidelong hit. It would not.

On the eastern shore of the United States, hurricane warnings had not yet been posted, and residents continued on with their daily lives, unaware of the killer heading their way.

1

Chapter One

It was a beautiful 4th of July, the air was warm, muggy, and the crowds were huge. Tourists all over the tri bay area, the Yacht club was full at lunch time, as was every other restaurant in the area, Gene Thomas was firing up the grill in the parking lot of the club, in anticipation of the community wide cookout the Cove hosted every year. Beside him on a tray was a portable radio, one he'd had since college days. He had it tuned to a station in Wilmington and was now listening to the noon news, as he readied the grill.

Suzanne took special pleasure in watching the foot traffic in and out of her antiques store, and up in the coffee bar. A big smile on her face, she sat in a lawn chair under a shade tree in the Yacht club parking lot. Dawg, as big as he was, was in her lap, a jaunty red, white, and blue bandanna tied around his neck. He was a local celebrity and seemed to bask in the attention.

Gene and Cassie's twins were home from their last year of college, working the crowds, and helping out wherever they were needed. Mostly, they assisted their dad as he cooked burgers and hot dogs to order, and Cassie had just come out of the dining room, carrying a large platter of hamburgers for the grill.

Steve opened a chair next to his wife, and sitting, gave her a big smile. "What's on your mind, love?"

"Just enjoying the day", she patted his knee. "The parade was nice, wasn't it?"

"Yep, looking forward to the fireworks tonight. My Lord, you ever seen this many people here? You can't move for folks getting' in the way, and Phil told me a little while ago that the Hawk's Nest is sold out until after Labor Day"

"Mm, Wanda must be hopping over there, did she ever get any kitchen help?'

Steve shook his head, "Not that I know of."

Just then a bicyclist zoomed past, nearly upsetting the table of paper ware for dining. Gene hollered after the man, but he was gone in a flash, turning in across the street at Brandan's bike rental shop.

His brother motioned for Steve to come to the grill, and when he got there, the two of them bent over to listen to the weather report Shaking his head, Steve returned to his chair and his wife.

"What is it the two of you were so intent on?"

"Hurricane coming this way, they think, reported to be a massive storm. They are thinking a lot of property damage with it..."

"Evacuations?" Suzanne asked.

"They'll know more of the trajectory this evening. "He patted her arm and flashed her a dazzling smile. "Don't worry that gorgeous head of yours about it, we get storms all the time here, we'll manage."

She chuckled," remember that storm we had the first time you and I ever spent any time together?"

Holding her hand Steve nodded. "Do I ever, you had invited me, a stranger to spend the night in your guest room, and the storm was so bad, you couldn't throw me out after you got mad at me. A memorable night if there ever was one!"

"Well,' she laughed," I had no idea your Elvis business was legitimate, I had never met anyone quite like you, Mr. Thomas."

He leaned over and kissed her forehead, "and I doubt you ever will, Mrs. Thomas.

Just then, the crowd began to gather for their food, and the Thomases tied Dawg to a tree, and got in line with them.

***

Watching the fireworks, as usual, from the front porch of the Thomas cottage on Eventide Lane, were Skank and Lorraine, the Thomas twins, along with their parents, Gene and Cassie, and Emily and Brandan Hawks and their three young children.

Oohs and aahs accompanied each fiery burst, and as the sky lit up, Steve would catch a glimpse of the tourists still mingling on the beach or walking the store fronts. Emily had enlisted one of Kevin McLaughlin's teenagers to run the cash register at the store, and Bullet Head continued to hold forth as the barista up in the coffee bar.

Business was good this fourth of July, with a record number of tourists in Beryl's Cove, and new residents and businesses coming in all the time.

It was only yesterday that Steve and Dawg had walked over to a new development that was taking shape on the hill behind the Hawks Nest Bed and Breakfast. Wanda and Phil had installed a large party gazebo in their backyard, right in line with all the construction, and Wanda was not pleased about it. She offered peace and tranquility to her overnight guests, and bulldozers and dump trucks did not make for a peaceful setting. She thought she might appeal to the town board for permission to erect a six-foot basket weave fence between her and the new housing development. Hortense Wilkerson's solution to Wanda's was to fire her shotgun at the big trucks, hoping to disable them. Mayor Mclaughlin suggested she stick to the squirrels.

Following the fireworks display, everyone disbursed, Suzanne retreated into the house, while Steve snapped on Dawgs leash, and the two of them headed for the park.

Steve loved to sit on a park bench at night, the soft glow from the old-fashioned globe lights that ringed the park., cast a warm glow on the entire area. Dawg laid at his feet, tongue hanging out, and resting from the exertion of the walk. The animal was getting old, and his energy level was slipping, so, his human parents took every care with him, making sure not to stress the dog more than was necessary. Elvis too, was aging, and had just recently been an overnight guest of the local vet. Looking with affection at his pet, Steve hoped that with tender, loving care, both Dawg and Elvis would have more years with them.

Deciding to carry the bulldog, Steve picked him up, and headed across the street to the Thomas cottage. It had been a long day, and he was as tired as Dawg was.

Walking up the front steps, he could still hear the revelers at the Captain's Table, and other spots around town, and he noticed lights still on at the Hawks Nest B-and-B, up on the hill. in the grand old Victorian house that had been home to the marvelous Brown twins. Putting Dawg back on solid ground, Steve marveled at how much the Cove had changed since he first sailed his boat into the harbor 15 years ago. Doing that and meeting the beautiful Suzanne Coldwell had changed his life and thank God for that, he mused.

Shutting the door behind them, he unsnapped Dawg's leash, turned out the lights, and headed upstairs to bed, and that beautiful wife of his. In a corner of the sunroom, Dawg and Elvis, with sighs and animal grunts, settled into an intertwined heap on the large pet bed. All was quiet, for now.

Chapter Two

Steve walked Dawg along the beach the next morning, letting the bulldog snuffle in the sand and dig to his heart's content.

The waves were choppy this morning, and the eastern sky had a distinct grayish tint to it. They had hurricanes all the time at the coast, but Steve was concerned about the one coming. Warnings and alerts had been posted throughout the media, and all one could get on the news this morning was the impending storm. He worried that everything would hold, already there were yachts being moved out of harm's way, into deeper water and anchored to buoys. Steve watched as Kevin McLaughlin, and some of the other merchants on the boardwalk put up plywood at their storefronts. He'd get up with Brandan later on about the antique store and coffee bar windows. He reasoned that Brandan ad Phil were busy at the bicycle shop and the Hawks Nest with those windows. Then, he remembered the bluff house, they'd have to get more plywood from Kevin for all of those wraparound windows. He rubbed his forehead thinking of all the preparations he had yet to make. Tugging gently on Dawgs leash, he thought it best to get back and start on them. As he turned toward the house, he saw Bullet Head approaching, a big grin on his face. The two friends sat together on the seawall.

Bullet Head was always amused by Dawgs antics, and this morning, he laughed out loud as the animal snooted and found some large stones to toss around. "That dog's more human than a lot of people," he opined, while lighting up one of his huge cigars.

"You're up mighty early this morning old friend," Steve said.

"Uh uh, just getting' home. Me and the little lady been out all night, here, there, everywhere. Nice supper clubs in the area, and the dancing goes on all the time." The little lady he referred to was the Police Chiefs secretary, Genevieve, whom Bullet Head took a liking to. They had been one another's constant companion now for about two years.

Steve nudged his old Navy buddy. "When you gonna make an honest woman of that gal, and marry her?"

"Nope, not the marryin' kind, Swabby. She has her place, and I have mine, and we're liking it that way. We do visit back and forth on occasion. Know what I mean?" The big man gave Steve another grin.

"So, what's up with you and the beast this morning?" He puffed on his cigar.

"I'm just thinking of all the plywood I need to have put on all these windows, Suzanne's place, our house, and the bluff House. I'm sitting here wondering when I can get Brandan to help me."

"Hell fire, Swabby, you don't need him. You got me. Let's, go. Get your rear in gear, and we'll get it done." He got up, tugged at Steve's shirt and pulled him up. "C'mon, I've heard this storm's gonna be a doozie, let's get it done. Got to cover your assets".

You could hear Bullet Head's raucous laughter all up and down the beach, as the two men, followed by Dawg, strode away towards the antique store.

***

It was up in the afternoon before Steve returned from covering windows on the antique store and the Bluff House. Bullet Head had returned to his beach house, and Dawg seemed exhausted just by watching the activity. He and Elvis snoozed in an air-conditioned corner of the sun room.

Suzanne put a club sandwich down in front of Steve's

place at the kitchen table. "Everything secure?" she asked

Munching on his lunch, her husband nodded. "The Bluff House has a lot of windows, and fortunately, Large Bear was on patrol and helped us with a couple of the bigger picture windows. If he hadn't lent us a hand we'd still be there. He took a big swallow of iced tea and asked for more. "What's the latest weather?"

"Noon news said the governor was declaring an emergency, and asked all tourists and coastal residents to leave. The forecasters are saying tonight, at high tide, the storm will hit."

Steve chewed his sandwich and looked at her. "Do you think we should leave?"

She shook her head and smiled at him. "This is our home, we'll see it through, there have been other storms and we've managed."

"We could go to the mountain house."

"No, we'll be okay…don't you think?"

Wiping his mouth, and declaring the club sandwich the best he ever ate, Steve nodded, and took her hand in his. "Of course we will."

The animals were getting restless, typical of their behavior at an approaching hurricane. The Thomas couple did their best to comfort their pets, and Steve said he thought he'd run across to the hardware store and get some batteries. "Just in case," he said.

As he walked across Seabreeze avenue, Suzanne watched and noticed the darkening clouds as the outer bands of the hurricane approached. Out on the highway, there was a steady stream of cars and campers as folks evacuated. She knew Skank and Rainey were staying in town for the duration, Skank had secured their island house plus their pet goat, Dolly. So Suzanne was secure in the knowledge they'd get though yet another coastal storm. Looking at the clouds and the quickening wind, she knew it would be a long night, a very long night.

Chapter Three

The hurricane hit during the night with 85-mile-per-hour winds, causing limbs to snap, awnings to bend, and signs to fall down. It rained so hard, you could not see the street. What signs Wanda and Phil had put up at their place blew across the road into a ditch. Boats rocked in the bay, and the railing of the yacht club came down and landed half-in and half-out of the ocean. Trash cans from yards littered the street, along with the dirt, limbs, and branches off of trees. One of Hortense Wilkerson's chickens lay dead in the road, its neck bent at an odd angle.

Unbeknownst to all, the storm hit Beryl's Island sending debris all across the Peterson's yard. Skank's newest runabout came loose and was tossed about, finally disappearing into the depths, as it sank offshore. His outbuildings blew away and one could hear dolly bleating in terror as the awnings flapped and tree limbs and trash lashed the side of the house.

The next morning, rising early, to survey the damage, Steve and Suzanne walked the property, one end to the other. They looked over the fencing, the gazebo, and one of Steve's sheds in the back was leaning precariously, the window blown out, and the door hanging by its hinges. He had secured them all, and it seemed they came through it with just minimal damage. He moved up the steps of the deck, opened the sunroom door, and brought out the porch furniture he had put inside the house. Sweeping off the debris from the deck was all it took to make the place good as new. Although a bad storm, this hurricane could have been much, much worse, and damage was minimal.

They brought the animals out for some play time, and Suzanne went to make coffee. The day following a hurricane is generally still, clear, and beautiful, and this day was no exception. While the Thomas couple drank their morning coffee, they listened as the town woke up and got to work. The noise of chainsaws was everywhere, as folks cut away broken limbs. Storekeepers along the boardwalk began to sweep in front of their business, and boat owners emerged to check on the various yachts that moored there. Up near the north bluff, Steve glimpsed the fishing boats that had been anchored in deep water. Some of the fishermen were weighing anchor, anxious to get to sea and capture the fish that had been stirred up by the storm. He watched as several of them made their way out to deep water.

Emily Hawks hollered from across the street that the antique store and coffee bar were okay, not to worry about them.

Dogs barked, and they could hear Hortense wailing in the distance over her dead chicken, then, firing her gun. Life had returned to normal in the Cove. As they sipped coffee, they heard Lorraine holler from a distance. Soon, she appeared in their yard, Elsie, her Irish Setter at her heels. She mounted the steps and flopped in a wicker chair.

"Girlfriend, I've had a night. Skank left early to go out to the island to check on things and animals, and Elsie here was upset all night." The three of them looked over at the big red dog, and saw she was fast asleep next to Dawg and Elvis. Elvis was actually underneath the pair of canines, all snoring soundly.

"Would you look at that," she laughed. "Sound asleep. Now why couldn't she have been that way last night, I had to put her in bed with us and, big as she is, she took up the entire thing. Between her and Skank, I had no room at all! Really starches my shorts."

Steve sipped his coffee, "any damage at your place, Rainey?"

"Not as I could tell, and I don't know about the island.

10

Reckon I'll find out when Skank gets home. You?"

Suzanne shook her head as she handed her best friend a cup of coffee. "We're good, and the store came thru okay, just a damaged awning, I think. That was some storm though."

Steve nodded, then mentioned that they had lost a window from the shed, and things were topsy turvy inside, but everything was accounted for.

As they spoke, Skank Peterson made his way back to Beryl's Cove, in his oldest, rundown, fishing boat, one arm dangling where it had been broken by a falling limb, as he stood inspecting the beach. On the seat beside him was a map he had found washed up by the storm. It was very old and looked to be a treasure map of some kind. He knew Rainey would have a hissy fit over his broken arm, and as soon as he had seen a doctor and got it set, he'd show the map to Steve.

True to form, Rainey screamed and hollered when she saw her husband, rushed to his side, and almost fainted with relief when she saw him. Leaving Elsie with the Thomases, she drove Skank to the walk-in clinic that was beside the post office, vowing to return as soon as they could get his arm tended to.

***

Two-and-a-half hours later, they returned, Skank sporting a brand new cast on his arm. The sling they gave him hung by his side, her husband telling Lorraine he was not wearing a sling.

After offering the couple, something cold to drink, Skank pulled a worn map from his pocket, and showed it to Steve. "What do you think?"

Turning it this way and that, he and Suzanne pored over the map. "Obviously a map of some sort. But look here. This bottom righthand corner is missing. What do I make of it? It's old, I mean very old, and quite obviously, a map leading somewhere. "

Yanking it out of Steve's hand Lorraine peered at it. "Why, of course, it's a treasure map! How wonderfully exciting. let's follow it and see where it goes."

"It's not complete, Rainey," Steve admonished," the whole bottom right hand quarter is missing. It's so old, it's probably nothing anyway."

"Yeah, maybe you're right. Well, let's go Skank." She turned to face her friends, while she snapped a leash on Elsie. "I need to get our patient home and make him rest. See ya'll tomorrow."

With that, they were down the back steps and across the yard, Suzanne began clearing glasses and Steve stared at the map lying on the glass topped table Something about it fascinated him, and it seemed to reach out to him. He picked it up and once more began to study it.

Chapter Four

Steve woke early, walked Dawg, fed the pets, and was making coffee when his wife entered the kitchen.

"Aren't you the early bird this morning", she said while she pecked him on the cheek "You're all dressed, are we going somewhere?" She petted the animals while she sipped the coffee Steve had made.

"Um, how's about we get on my cycle, and we tear around this place, and see what we can see?'

She laughed and looked at him while she buttered her toast. "You're fascinated with that map, aren't you? Do you really think it's any good and there might possibly be 'treasure' buried somewhere in the cove?"

Steve gave her sheepish grin. "Well, one never knows, but it might be fun to follow it and see where it goes, don't you think? It'll be a whole lot easier to follow it on our bike than try and get the car into tight places. Look here." He took the map and spread it out in front of her. "See here? These are woods. We can't get the car thru there. Waddya say, gorgeous? You up for an adventure?"

***

Twenty minutes later, they were astride Steve's Gold Wing motorcycle, heading away from the house. They didn't try and speak as they turned towards the woods that lay beyond the Happy Joe place on the north bluff. They rode until they emerged from the other side. So, finding nothing of interest, they remounted and headed out towards the strip mall on the highway. Behind the mall were woods, thick woods that ran for the entire 18 miles before coming out on Pykes Bay, one of the three towns in the Pikes County tri-bay area.

The deeper into the woods they went, the cooler it was, and Suzanne was enjoying the respite from the coastal heat and humidity.

Steve stopped suddenly and pointed off toward a particularly thick copse of trees. "Look, in that grove of trees, see anything?"

She peered over to where he was pointing. "Hmm, just barely making out some kind of...hm, yeah, it's a cabin, I think. Wonder how long it's been here. I never saw it before, have you?"

Steve shook his head. "No, but we've never been this far in before. You ever come here as a child?" he asked her.

Laughing now, Suzanne told him she was never allowed to come here. "Legend goes, it's haunted. That's why there is nothing between us and Pykes Bay. No builder has ever wanted to touch this place. Gives me the creeps just looking at it."

They dismounted, and Steve secured their helmets while he kept an eye on the somewhat rundown cabin. "Let's go check it out." He grabbed her hand and started forward, much to his wife's objections.

As they neared the cabin, they saw evidence of an extinguished fire and Steve saw an old, dilapidated pickup truck at the rear of the place. Just as they approached the vehicle, the back door swung open, and a small bespectacled mixed-race man suddenly opened the door.

"Well, hello there! Are you looking for something or someone in particular?" he asked.

Suzanne detected a strong British accent from the man. "N-no, we're just adventuring. Who are you?" She held tightly to Steve's hand, not sure of what was going to happen.

The Englishman motioned them to come inside. "Do step into my lair, won't you? He held out his hand to Steve and, shaking hands, told them his name. "Anderson Farnsworth here. Do come in."

Once inside, the Thomas couple saw a man about the same age as Farnsworth sitting in a wheelchair right next to the fireplace. "Won't you have a seat? Now then," he looked at them, "what brings you to our humble abode."

Steve looked from one man to the other, "I hardly know where to begin. We're the Thomases, Steve and Suzanne. How long you two been here?" he inquired.

Farnsworth waved the question away, "Oh, not long. What brings you two into the woods today?"

Steve cleared his throat and gazed at his wife. She looked terrified. "Just cruising on the motorcycle, and we came across this cabin, I don't remember it ever being here before. Where you guys from, anyway?"

"Now see here, Thomas, I'm not unfriendly, but I fail to see it's any of your business. However, I don't wish to be rude either. We are simply summering here and, due to a lack of lodging, we came upon this humble cabin so we're here, at least until, what you chaps call Labor Day.

Steve and Suzanne nodded in unison. "Oh. What do you do back in England?"

Clearly wary now of his intruders. Farnsworth could not hide his frustration. "Again, I can't understand why you'd want to know but, anyway, I matriculate at Cambridge—I teach Baroque Bassoon, and James here is merely my traveling companion. Now, may I fix you some tea?" He stood up and headed for a rundown wood stove in the corner that was vented through the roof.

Suzanne had never let go of Steve's hand and she rose suddenly, declaring that they really had to get on their way but, by golly, it was great meeting them. The two were out the door and on their motorcycle before Farnsworth could even get off his chair.

As they roared away from the cabin, and back toward town, Suzanne asked Steve if he believed the man.

"Not a word," he said.

Farnsworth, and Trilby, now both standing at the window, the wheelchair abandoned in a corner, watched as the couple rode off.

"Where are we going now, Steve?"

"To see Chief Nathan Sowinski!"

Chapter Five

"Baroque Bassoon? What the hell is that?" Chief Nathan Sowinski turned from the window in his office to face the Thomas couple. "I never heard of such a thing, Steve. You sure about that?"

Steve shrugged. "All I can do is tell you what the man said, Nathan, Baroque Bassoon. At Cambridge."

"England?"

The couple nodded together.

Sowinski took his place behind the desk and scribbled some notes on a pad. "What else?"

"Well," Steve began, "there was another man there with him, in a wheelchair, but I don't think he's handicapped."

"Why is that?"

"The man's leg muscles were too well defined for a man who is confined to a wheelchair. Suzanne noticed that as well."

The chief knew that, as an amateur detective, Steve's instincts were pretty good, and he learned years ago to pay attention to them. "Okay, what else? What did these men look, like?"

Clearing her throat, Suzanne took over the conversation. "The English guy, Anderson Farnsworth, was small, mixed-race, and wiry. His companion was big, probably tall, muscular, and had large, bulging eyes. He creeped me out if you want to know the truth, Chief. Never said a word. Did he, hon?"

"This other man have a name?"

Her husband shook his head no, "No—wait a minute, it was James something." He paused and looked to his wife.

"Trilby," Suzanne added. "James Trilby. Farnsworth never said what this Trilby guy did, other than be a companion for him."

"And you say they were living in this old cabin? Must

have been the old Philip's place. That cabin's been abandoned for years, since old man Philips died. He was a notorious moonshiner. Been in jail couple times for sellin' the stuff on the coast. Arthur Morgan told me they never could rehabilitate the man."

Suzanne recalled the many stories her dad had told her about the previous chief and his battles with Philips. She smiled at the memory.

"They may have been living there, Nathan, but from what I saw of the sparse furnishings, it was hardly comfortable. They had a tea kettle of water steaming on the old wood stove, but we saw no real signs of living in the place."

"Hmmm. How did you happen to come across these characters, anyway?"

"Here." Steve unfolded the map from his pocket. "Skank ran across this thing floating in the water when he went out to the island to check on their place after the hurricane."

The chief studied the map and, nodding at his visitors, remarked, "Well, I'll be. This would take you right to the place. It's old though. Lord knows how long it's been around."

"You think it belonged to old man Philips?"

Nathan turned the map this way and that, studying it. "Possible. He was supposed to have made some money off his shine. At least that's what Arthur Morgan told me." Handing the map back to Steve, he asked what they were going to do next.

"I'm following it. It might be fun. Besides, I got nothing else to do."

Nathan scratched his head. "Skank goin' with you?"

"Naw, this is his busy season. Me and Suzanne will check it out. We got a month yet before we leave for the mountains. We'll see where it goes."

On the walk home, they held hands. "Where to now, hon?" Suzanne asked.

"Wrightsville beach. Can you get away for a day or two, maybe?"

"When it comes to being with my best guy, you betcha. I'll speak to Emily and Bullet Head both this afternoon. Tell them we'll be away and to watch the fort for me. How 'bout running the guys over to Rainey's for me while I slip across the street to the store."

"Oh, they'll love it, especially Elvis. He delights in tormenting that dog of theirs." He bent down and kissed her. Suzanne headed for the antique store while Steve prepared to pack up the animals and dropped them off at their Auntie Rainey's.

He chuckled to himself as he thought about what fun this adventure was going to be, a real treasure map!

***

An hour later, they were ready to leave when a knock at the front door interrupted them. Steve opened the door to find Phil Hawks standing there with a small valise. Running up the sidewalk was Rainey, also with a small case in hand.

"What's this? Phil, Rainey?"

"We're going with you, Steve, and that's that!" She elbowed her way inside and hugged her best friend, Suzanne "Well, are you going to stand there or are we leaving?" Lorraine Bracket had always been a formidable person, but according to Steve, this took the cake.

Phil stepped inside also. "Emily told us about the map. So I figured Wanda can handle the Hawks Nest. I want to be a part of this adventure, Steve, and as for Rainey," he cast her a disdainful look," Lord knows what she's doing here."

"Hey, that's not nice, Phil. It was my husband who found the map. Naturally, I should be a party to this." She pouted at him.

"If I may ask something," Suzanne put in, "who's

minding the store, Rainey, and what about Dawg and Elvis?"

Rainey shook her red curls, "My secretary, Sharon can run the office for a couple, days. I have no showings scheduled and she'll watch the animals till Skank comes back in this afternoon. Now, let's stop talkin' about it, and move. Out. The. Door!"

With a shake of his head, Steve gave them each a smile, and led the way to the garage, and ten minutes later, they were headed out of town.

From the shadows behind the Thomas cottage, Anderson Farnsworth and James Trilby watched as Steve guided their car out of town. Parked on a side street, the two headed for their own vehicle, and started off.

Chapter Six

After a ferry ride, and a check of the map that Phil held for Steve, they rode thru downtown Wilmington, and headed for Wrightsville beach. Traffic was heavy, as it always is in July, but following Phil's direction, they pulled into the parking lot of the Blockade Runner Hotel.

"This can't be right, Phil," Lorraine whined from the back seat. "This is a hotel, probably not even here when that map was drawn."

"Exactly," Steve added. "That's why we need to check it out. Let me see that map, Phil."

Spreading the map out as best he could, Steve studied it. Turning it this way and that, he gazed off in the distance and shook his head. Refolding the map, he looked at his passengers.

"According to this, we have to hunt on the beach for something buried approximately 50 yards on the lee side of the hotel. Let's go."

Leaving their bags in the trunk, the four of them trudged around the side of the Blockade resort and made their way to the beach. The sand was thick, and made walking difficult, plus, the water lapped at their shoes with every breaking wave. Taking their shoes off and rolling up the cuffs of their pants, the group went in different directions, looking for whatever they thought would hide whatever it was they were looking for.

After an hour of scouring the beach, they gave up and, dodging tourists, sat on some grass at the edge of the hotel property.

Steve ran his hand through his hair. "I don't think this is going to work, folks, we need some uninterrupted time to really search this place. Let's figure out something to do until dark and we'll come back late tonight and give it another try."

Just at that moment, a family throwing a Frisbee around sailed it over Phil's head and it landed in the ocean. Phil grabbed at it before it could be carried out to sea and a young boy around twelve ran up and thanked him for retrieving it.

Waving his hand toward the crowd, Steve chimed in, "See what I mean? We need to be alone to hunt whatever it is we're looking for."

Wiping her face with a hankie, Rainey began to fan herself. "I don't know about you all, but this sun is cooking me. Let's check in, have a nice dinner, and try late tonight."

The other three just stared at her for a moment. "What?"

Suzanne laughed at her friend. "Rainey, that's the best idea you've had all day."

***

"Sir, you've got to be kidding! This is July. We're booked solid and have been for several months now. You are welcome to eat dinner in our dining room, but booking a room is out of the question. Sorry."

He reached for the phone that was ringing and, nodding his head, the desk clerk looked up at Steve's party. He hung up, and addressed them again. "You're in luck, a guest in one of our street side rooms has suffered a heart attack. They are taking him to the hospital now. If you want to wait, we can clean the room for you and you can check in about 8:00. It is the only available space I have and I can assure you there is no other room available in the entire beach area.

The four of them looked to one another and collectively shrugged their shoulders. Steve asked the desk what sort of room it was.

"Nothing fancy. One queen bed, a sofa, and desk chair, but it does have a nice bathroom with it. Looks out on the street." He was interrupted by the ringing telephone again and paused to answer it. Momentarily he covered the receiver and spoke again to Steve. "Take it or leave it, mister. This caller wants to know if we have a cancellation. The room is his, if you don't want it."

"We'll take it."

The clerk gave him the room key with a smirk at the women and told them they could check in after dinner.

With a sigh, they left the lobby and headed towards the dining room. Rainey was still fanning herself and Phil was wobbling as he walked, trying to work the sand out of his trousers.

Chapter Seven

Despite Rainey's protestations, Steve would not give up his side of the bed. He and Suzanne wanted to get a few hours sleep before returning to the beach in the middle of the night. So they sacked out, leaving Rainey to fold her 5'9" frame onto a love seat and Phil trying to bend his 6'2" body into the bathtub for some shuteye.

Steve woke with a start and saw that it was 1:00 a.m. Quietly, he woke the others. Dressing hurriedly, they skipped the elevator, and took the utility stairs to the door opening onto the small patch of grass that led to the beach. Steve carried a flashlight and they began to scan the widest area they could at water's edge, Rainey complaining of the sand and debris hurting her feet the whole time. Finally, she sat down on a large boulder off to the side and, exhausted, she watched the waves come in. The others dug, scratched, and moved sand around, looking for whatever it was they were supposed to find. Rainey pushed her hair behind her ear and watched.

Phil eventually joined her on the rock, and shook his head, "I don't think there's anything here, do you?"

"Naw, just a wild goose chase, if you ask me—still, it would be nice to find a treasure. What do you think it is, Phil?"

He shrugged, "Haven't a clue, Wanda thinks it will be confederate money."

"Useless."

"You got that right," he added.

Daybreak was barely on the horizon when Steve and Suzanne found their companions sitting together. "How long you two been there," he inquired.

Lorraine answered him, "Not more n' hour, why?"

"Get up!"

"What?"

"Get up! Phil, help me move this boulder aside."

"You gotta be kidding, buddy. It must weigh a ton." He and Rainey stood up, stepping out of the way, even as they protested.

"C'mon," Steve shouted, "put your shoulder to it!"

The two men pushed as hard as they could, moving the rock only slightly. So Steve told the women to join as well. The four of them pushed and heaved, finally shoving the rock aside and looking into the indentation it left. They began to dig with their hands.

"We'd better hurry, the tide's coming in."

"Look", Suzanne pointed down the beach, and the group saw a couple out early walking their dog.

Quickly, they all turned and sat on the rock, appearing to be two couples enjoying the sunrise. Soon, they were back to digging, when Phil let out a shout. "I found something!"

He brought up a small, tin box, rusted and bent, but with an effort, they pried the lid off, and unfolded a piece of paper from inside.

Rainey was impatient, "What's it say? What's it say?"

Steve shone his flashlight on it and read: "You found yourself by the sea, now, go and read where next you need to be".

"Holy smoke, what's that supposed to mean?"

Suzanne stared off at the open water. She was pensive when she turned to the group and offered her opinion. "Where would you go to read something like a map, maybe?"

Collectively, the others shrugged.

"The library, naturally."

"Darling, you're a genius!" Steve kissed her, and suggested they all go get cleaned up, have some breakfast, and head to the library. *I doubt they open before9:00. We've got plenty of time, he reasoned.*

It was a motley-looking, wet and sandy bunch that trudged through the lobby to the elevator that morning, causing stares and snickers as they headed upstairs. Steve wondered what the cleaning women would think when they found Phil's sleeping nest in the bathtub. He was chuckling to himself as he opened the door to their room just as his cell, phone rang. It was Nathan, with disturbing news.

Chapter Eight

"Are you sure, Nathan? Who found him, and how did he get there?"

"Sure as we can be, Steve. We found identification on him and he matches the description the missus gave us. When you get back, we'll go over all the details. Take care."

Nathan signed off and Steve gave a concerned look.

"What?" they asked in unison.

"That large drainage ditch behind the Hawks Nest, the one they hope will be leveled for a parking lot or something. They found the body of James Trilby in it as it began to drain from the hurricane. He's dead."

They all spoke at once, asking how, why, and who did it. Steve had no answers for them and suggested they get on with the task at hand.

After getting directions to the local library and checking out, Steve made a couple of wrong turns but eventually pulled up in front of the modern, low-slung building that housed the library. As the four of them climbed the few steps to the entrance, they did not notice the man sitting, watching them from his car at the curb, a sly smirk across his face.

"Miss," Steve began, "we're wanting the archive room or some room that has maps in it."

Without looking up, the librarian pointed up the half story steps to her right.

Phil flipped the light switch and looked at the array of atlases and books in front of them. "Holy smoke, where do we begin in this place?"

Rainey shook her head in amazement, "We'll never find what we want in all this stuff. I say we call it quits and go home."

"Come *on* guys, you wanted an adventure, and we got it.

What harm could it do to spend a couple hours searching thru this material? Besides, it's cool in here. He grabbed a North Carolina atlas and handed it to Rainey, gave Phil a big book of maps, and he and Suzanne each took an atlas. They sat at the big study table and began going through all of it.

Three hours, and many volumes of material, later they were growing bleary-eyed. Rainey pushed away from the table, stood up, stretched, and yawned. She whipped out her compact to have a look at herself.

"Would you just look at the mess I'm in," she whined. "It just starches my shorts to have my makeup and hair a mess! I'm hungry, Steve. Can we go and get something to eat?" She walked around the room, moving her arms back and forth to bring the circulation back.

Suzanne picked up her heavy atlas to return it to the shelf, when a slip of paper fell from the inside lining.

"Whoa, what's this?" She picked it up and unfolded it. "Listen to this. "This is fun. See how much longer you can run?" In a corner of the paper, were the letters ESE.

"What's that supposed to mean?" Rainey cried.

Steve and Phil sat back down, facing one another. "ESE, Phil, east by southeast?"

"That's my guess."

"Who's doing this anyway?" asked Rainey

"Well," Steve began, "someone wants us to find something hidden, and these clues, I guess, will lead us to it. They would mean nothing to anyone not following the trail like we are. Just gibberish to anyone else."

"It's starting to be gibberish to me" Rainey said, as she smoothed her hair down.

"East by southeast, is back our way. What say we go get some lunch and then, be on the road. If we hurry, we can make the late afternoon ferry."

"Now you're talkin'," "Phil added, as he turned off the light and shut the door.

Chapter Nine

After dropping his passengers off at home, Steve drove over to the police station and walked into the chief's office.

"Steve! Back so, soon from the treasure hunt? What d'ya find?"

"Well, nothing so far. And Rainey and Phil were getting antsy, so we came back home. We'll pick up the trail later. Tell me about Trilby."

"Not much to tell, really. Body's in Raleigh at the ME's office, but we didn't find any visible signs of violence. Could be he drowned in that big hole. The water had to be a good six or seven feet. You seen that hole over behind the Hawks Nest. It's huge."

"Where's Farnsworth?" Steve asked.

"Nobody knows. 'Course, nobody but you and Suzanne even knew the man was here to begin with. Nobody has seen him, nobody has heard of him, and there is no sign he was even here."

"The cabin?"

"Clean as a whistle," Nathan added. "You'd never know anyone was ever in the place."

Steve shook his head in puzzlement. "This just doesn't make sense, Nathan. I know what we saw. Reckon he's even English?"

The chief shot him a funny look, "What do you think?"

"Well, you find out anything, Suzanne and I would really like to know."

"Will do, Steve, where you headed now?"

"Home, I want to study our clues some more."

Five minutes later, he walked through his office into the living room where his wife sat reading the paper, Elvis

29

comfortable in her lap. He sat in his lounge chair and studied his pets, both fast asleep.

"What d'ya find out about Trilby?"

"Not a thing, and there isn't a trace of Farnsworth anyplace."

"So, what's next?" she asked him.

He pulled some crumpled papers from his pocket and spread them out in his lap. "I'm going to study these clues and see if I can figure them out. Somebody has gone to a lot of trouble, and I'd like to know why and how long these clues have been hidden. They could have been in place a hundred years or more. Do you think this is even worth pursuing, Hon?"

Suzanne smiled at her husband. "That's hard to say, Love. If it gives you, pleasure, then I'd say it's worth the effort."

Their thoughts were interrupted by a knock at the front door. Steve opened it to find Phil standing there. "C'mon in."

Phil nodded to Suzanne and asked to examine the paper with the last clue on it. "This is fun. See how far you can run, ESE," he read. He scratched his head. "You know, guys, when you draw a line from the library in Wrightsville Beach, straight line East by Southeast, it takes you to the marina at Baylor's Point. Right smack in the middle of it. What say we scope it out?"

"Now?"

"Why not? Wanda's busy setting up some rooms for our next guests and I just saw Rainey out jogging towards town. We could round her up in no time. Obviously, we have nothing else to do, so let's go."

The Thomases raised an eyebrow, and stared at their guest, finally nodding an assent. Suzanne put Elvis on the floor, disappointing him tremendously. He stretched, yawned, and gave her a dirty look before skulking off in search of Dawg.

The Tri Bay area was founded during the Civil war, when

the region served as a way station for the Underground Railway. Tunnels under the chapel that sat on the hill overlooking the town were a holding area where the runaway slaves awaited a ship that would take them to Canada and freedom. The Tri Bay refers to the towns of Pyke's Bay, Beryl's Cove, and Baylor's Point, each town between 18 and 38 miles apart. The greatest distance was separating Baylor's Point and Beryl's Cove.

In the back seat of Steve's car were Phil, and Rainey, still in her jogging shorts and tank top, her hair a matted, sweaty mess around her face. She was unhappy with her looks and hoped her dark sunglasses would disguise her enough that no one would recognize her as they drove out of town. As luck would have it, Hortense Wilkerson's niece, Shelley, was visiting and, recognizing the group, gave a smile and a wave as she left the post office.

It took Steve a little more than forty-five minutes to reach Baylor's Point, a beautiful, hilly town, with jaw dropping views of the Atlantic Ocean. Upscale homes, elaborate resort hotels, and motels dotted the shoreline. Steve quickly located the marina and pulled into a parking place.

"What are we looking for?" Rainey asked.

"Don't rightly know," she was told, "just look for an outcropping, a loose brick, or a large boulder that looks out of place. Let's go. Separate and we'll cover more ground that way."

After two hours of endless digging and snooping, they came up empty-handed. Phil was disappointed, while Rainey whined that she was starving to death.

"Let's go inside and get lunch and continue looking afterward," was Phil's suggestion.

"I can't go into a yacht club looking like, this!" Rainey cried. "For Pete's sake, isn't there a burger joint nearby?"

Steve put his arm around her shoulder. "Come on, Red. Leave your sunglasses on and no one will see you."

Rainey and Suzanne walked ahead of the men. Phil was chuckling over Steve's suggestion to Rainey. Both men shook their head in laughter as they entered the cooled dining room.

***

Lunch was leisurely and, as the men devoured huge ice cream sundaes for dessert, the two women looked out at the beautiful bay. It was a peaceful day. The sun was high and bright in the sky, the ocean relatively calm, and, while Baylor's Point did have some touristy shops, most of the residents were summer dwellers, having homes or condos in the area. An occasional tourist, toting a surfboard or cooler would make their way down to the public beach. The others enjoyed the hotel and motel pools or their own private swimming pool.

After their lunch, the four friends stood on the beach, scanning the horizon. "Logistically, Phil, do you think we're any closer?"

The map was produced and spread out on a huge rock, where they could all examine it. Steve peered closely at the line Phil had drawn from Wrightsville to where the marina was located.

"According to this, we need to walk a little further north."

Nodding in that direction, the four of them took off, walking about seventy-five yards due north. The beach was more secluded there and, as each one of them scanned the area, they failed to see the man sitting in his car up on the road, his face behind a newspaper he was holding. Finally, he smiled to himself, put the car in gear, and drove away, happy with the thought the group would eventually find another bit of direction.

Finally, it was Rainey, who spotted it: an ancient, rusty anchor half-buried in the sand up a slight incline from where they stood. Weeds and sea grass had almost obliterated it from view.

"C'mon, let's start digging!"

The anchor was pretty well wedged in the ground, but with a monumental effort, they moved it enough to see the big hole underneath. Some more digging and Steve brought up another small, metal box, similar to the one they had found back in Wrightsville.

They looked up in time to see a security guard heading their way. Steve grabbed the box and the four of them headed as fast as they could to the car. Speeding off, they looked behind to see the guard, hands on hips, watching them drive away.

Steve did not stop until he pulled up to his own garage back in Beryl's Cove.

They entered the kitchen thru Steve's office, placed the box on the table, and Suzanne fetched a screwdriver from under the sink. Breaking into the box Steve pulled out a dirty, crumpled piece of paper and read it to the others "Across the sea you will be, in a bay that you can see."

Collective groans all around.

"What does that mean, I wonder?" Rainey said.

"Steve," Phil began, "do you think this is simply a wild goose chase? Someone having fun with us?"

Shrugging, Steve shook his head. "Let me ponder on these clues overnight and we can start in again in the morning, if that's okay. I'm kinda bushed from all that digging, anyway."

The others went home and, after showering off all the sand they had accumulated, the Thomas couple sat on the deck, watching the sunset over the water.

Steve was definitely puzzled, and with the clues spread out before him, attempted to make sense of all of it.

Chapter Ten

At 8:30 the next morning, Chief Nathan Sowinski was at their back door. Suzanne ushered him into the kitchen, and offered him a cup of coffee and a cinnamon bun.

"What's up??" Steve bit into his pastry, offering Dawg a small bite.

" I asked the ME to put a rush on the autopsy of Trilby and he just emailed me. The victim had a king-sized gash on the back of his head. ME thinks it happened before he fell into the water hole."

"So, he didn't drown?" Suzanne questioned.

"Oh, he drowned all right. The cold water more than likely roused him somewhat. He took a big breath and that was that. I'm wondering if this Farnsworth chap might have been the one to kill him."

"Still no word on his whereabouts, Chief?" Steve slipped another morsel to Dawg, who happily snapped it up.

Nathan put down his coffee cup, and shook his head." Nary a word, and I have APB's out all over the place. Anything else you remember about him, it might help;."

Suzanne looked from one to the other, "His hair," she said. "It didn't look real."

"You mean a toupee?"

She nodded. "Exactly."

Steve was astonished. "You never mentioned this to me, Hon."

She half-laughed. "Well, I didn't think it was important at the time."

Nathan wiped his mouth, thanked them for the hospitality, and said he'd add it to the APB, along with the fact that Farnsworth may or may not have a British accent. He paused at the doorway and looked back at them. "How goes the treasure hunt?" He laughed.

Steve flashed his brightest smile. "For now, it doesn't, Chief, and Phil even thinks it could be a wild goose chase."

"Well, could be. Then again, it could be something. You never know." Laughing, he turned to go, remembered something, and came back. "Forgot to mention that my brother Paul and his band are playing a gig at the yacht club in two weeks. Mid-Summer Bash it's called."

"We'll be there" Steve called after him. "Gonna go look something up on the computer, Suze. I'll be in the office if you need me."

***

Nathan stood looking out his office window at all the activity going on in town. Suddenly, he saw Hortense Wilkerson and her niece Shelley crossing the street, walking towards his office. Before he could retrieve his cap and leave, they were both standing in front if the his desk.

"Got a complaint, chief," Hortense intoned.

Rubbing his forehead, Nathan hunched his shoulders, muttering to himself, "Kinda thought you did." Looking up, he smiled and offered then a seat. "What can I do for you?"

"I want a man arrested," Hortense laid her shotgun on the floor as she spoke. "Some foreigner stopped this morning and told me it was illegal to shoot squirrels in the city limits and said he was going to have me locked up if I didn't stop! The very nerve of the man, not even from round here either." She was indignant as she spoke.

"And you want me to have him arrested?"

"For harassin' an upstandin', tax-paying citizen. Now, go get him."

Nathan leaned back, shaking his head, wondering what in the world he was going to do with this woman.

"Not only that," Hortense continued, "he was eyeballin'

35

Shelley here in a way I don't cotton to."

The chief smiled, "Well, she is a beautiful woman Hortense."

Hortense stomped her foot and raised her gun, "Course she's beautiful. She's got my genes coursing thru her body. Now, what do you aim to do about it, and when?"

Nathan was trying hard to control himself, but couldn't help chuckle over the reference to Hortense's beautiful genes. He shrugged and waved his hand over his face. "I don't see wha—"

"He was English," Shelley added.

That stopped the chief. "English? Did he give a name. What direction did he head out to and what did he look, like?"

"No name, short, skinny, and bald as an egg, and," she pointed towards the south bluff. "That way."

Before she could finish, Nathan had grabbed his cap and headed out.

Hortense and her niece traded looks. "Now what got him so fired up all of a sudden?"

***

The police car screeched to a stop in front of the Thomas house. Letting himself in through Steve's office, he found the man at his computer, and motioned for him to follow. "Got a lead," he said over his shoulder.

Back in the car, they headed the few blocks out to the south bluff, where the two men stood overlooking the huge hole that had been flooded in the hurricane. Nothing but mud and debris was left now as they studied the hole in the ground. Nathan explained to Steve about Hortense's visit and the man she said was English.

"So, what are we looking for, Chief?"

"Anything that shouldn't be here." He was standing on the very edge of the hole. "My word, but that is one giant crater."

He looked up and could see the back end of the Hawks' property 100 yards away. Beyond the Hawk's Nest was the town of Beryl's Cove. "Not sure Wanda has a case against the construction company, unless she's wanting to expand her place into some kind of entertainment venue."

"I think that's what she has in mind, Chief. What's this crater for, anyway?"

"S'posed to be the start of the foundation and sewage pipes for that condo complex the builders want. In addition, I think they are going to put some small specialty shops in here."

Steve nodded. "Mae Ruth and Jack won't like that. They have the biggest house out here on the bluff, not to mention our bluff house, the one for the arts center guests. And your own home is out this way. Buster and Mildred's place too. What do you think about it all?"

Nathan pushed his cap to the top of his head, and continued to look around the area. "Well, my friend, I learned long ago that you can't stop progress. We get an injunction against the builder. They'll just go somewhere else, maybe even a more congested area. This entire area is growing. We have to go with it, or we stifle."

Steve nodded and joined him as they walked back to the police cruiser.

"Didn't see a thing, did you? At least we know your Englishman is still here—somewhere."

Chapter Eleven

What had started out as a few friends enjoying a silly, friendly treasure hunt had grown. Phil mentioned it to Brandan, his son. Brandon and Emily saw Hortense and Shelley out, so they mentioned it to them. Hortense spoke to Genevieve and Genevieve, on a day she was having her hair done, told Mona at the beauty parlor all about it. And Brandan told Bullet Head all about it one morning.

The next day following the chief and Steve's visit to the large crater that was arousing so much attention, Brandan, Bullet Head, and Shelley showed up at the Thomas' door, just as Phil and Rainey were arriving. No sooner had they gained admittance to the Thomas cottage, than Large Bear, the biggest human being anyone had ever known, showed up in his monster pickup truck.

"Reasoned we would need some major transportation to go treasure hunting," was his explanation.

Exasperated, Steve explained that it may be nothing at all, just a ruse, or they might find something valuable, no one knew.

"That's okay, Steve, we got nothing else to do, and it does sound like fun. Something I haven't done since childhood."

There was general assent all around. So, one by one, they all piled into Large Bear's truck, the women inside, the men riding in the cargo bay.

"Where to?" Large Bear asked.

Steve silently read the last clue to himself, and shaking his head, and shrugging his shoulders, told the group they'd head over to Pyke's Bay. They all groaned, but they were also clueless as to where else to go. So, Large Bear turned around and headed towards the last bay in the tri bay area.

"Haven't we been here before?" Rainey whined.

"Maybe", Phil said, "they missed something. There's more of us this time. We can spread out further."

Once the bay came into view, Steve told Large Bear to get close to the beach. After unloading the passengers, they all scattered. No one noticed the bald headed man who sat watching them from his car across the street. Once he was sure they were hunting seriously, he drove off, a smile on his face.

After almost forty minutes of searching, when Brandan held up a dirty, brown bottle with a cork in the top and what looked like a piece of wadded up paper inside. The group was excited and gathered around as Brandan opened the bottle and pulled out the paper.

"Tell us what is says!" Shelley was excited now. This was more exciting than sitting with her Aunt Hortense, watching her shoot squirrels.

Unfolding the paper, Brandan read, "Closer to home now. Get there, and I'll show you how."

"What the devil, does that mean Steve?"

Pausing only a moment, Steve looked at his assembled friends. "The only place we haven't looked, Beryl's Cove."

"You mean, after all this time, we're going back home?"

"Looks like it," Large Bear added, while ushering them all back towards his truck.

Steve held back, taking Suzanne's arm keeping her with him.

"What is it?"

"We've been set up, Suze."

"How do you know?"

"When we were here before, we searched this area thoroughly, that bottle was not here. Also, that paper looked fairly clean, not like it had been in a bottle for a lengthy time."

"Are you sure, Sweetheart?"

"Positive," he answered.

"But who, why, and to what end?"

"I have no idea, look, Large Bear is motioning for us to come on, we'll talk at home."

Chapter Twelve

It was decided on the way home, that the women would search the shoreline and the men would go out to the highway and search from one side of the city limits, to the other. If nothing was found, they'd all begin to move towards the inner town.

After an hour in the sun, the women sought shelter under some trees at water's edge. Mopping her face, Suzanne and Shelley were just about ready to call it a day when Large Bear's truck appeared, the men spilling from it.

"We found something!" Brandan was shouting, while waving a piece of paper that Large Bear kept trying to take from him.

Finding a large boulder, the paper was opened and spread out before the group.

"Why, that's a map of the underground tunnel beneath Mariner's Chapel!" Rainey grabbed Suzanne by the arm. "Remember that creepy British couple that was stealing stuff and hiding in there years ago, and we had a murderous librarian along with it."

Shelley looked quizzically at the group. Phil smiled and explained the caper to her. "Our former police chief, Arthur Morgan even dubbed it the case of the murderous librarian," Rainey added.

"Mount up, let's ride." Large Bear motioned the group towards his truck.

Once at the tunnel, which ran under the church though the opening was behind, Pastor Kapas joined the group in their search for the short, iron handle that lifted the lid off the tunnel entrance.

Stale, musty air greeted the group as they slowly

descended the earthen steps inside. "We can't see a thing," the minister said. "Wait here and I'll go up to my office and grab a flashlight."

"I've got a mag light in the truck. Be right back," and Large Bear was gone.

While they waited, Steve and Rainey explained about the tunnel being a stop on the underground railroad during the Civil War. "Ships at sea would be signaled from the mound out there, come by and pick up the slaves, and carry them to freedom in Canada. It's a very interesting story, really."

Suzanne added to the story. "We tried to make this tunnel a tourist attraction, but there was absolutely no interest. So we closed it back up again."

"Kapas and Large Bear returned almost at the same time, and the group moved forward, looking around on the ground. They decided they probably needed to dig, and search.

"The garden shed out back. Be right back," and Kapas was up and out of the tunnel once again.

"I'm getting hungry," Rainey complained.

"Well, we're here. Let's just end this thing, then we'll go get a good lunch."

By then, Pastor Kapas was back, and the men began to move some earth, hoping to find—*something.*

After several long minutes of digging, here and there, Phil was shoveling and heard a "clink" as he did so. Just as he was about to bring up a metal box, they heard heavy footsteps behind them. Turning to see who it was, Suzanne gasped, and Steve stood up and faced the man,

"Farnsworth!"

"The name's Mitchell and I'm not British, as you can tell. I'll take the strongbox now."

Steve moved forward, but before he could reach the intruder Mitchell was up the steps and gone, shutting the entrance behind him. To the group, it sounded like he was putting a lock on the iron handle that opened the place.

Phil joined him, and the two men, with Large Bear helping, tried to push open the earthen door.

"We're stuck, I'm afraid."

Collectively, they took out cell phones, and tried to get a signal, but that was futile, the ground was too dense. So, they sat down and tried to figure a way out.

Rainey began to cry.

Chapter Thirteen

Police Chief Nathan Sowinski sat at his desk, a cold cup of coffee on the credenza behind him. He was reading the papers from the FBI that Genevieve had just put in front of him. Not five minutes later, his secretary was back, pointing out the window Nathan turned to see Hortense Wilkerson heading straight for his door.

"Oh lawd, batten down the hatches, here comes trouble!"

Hortense entered his office, her shotgun aimed right at his midsection. Nathan stood up and pointed a finger at here.

"Now Hortense, put that blunderbuss away. Don't you be pointing that thing at me or anyone else, or I'll throw your skinny butt in jail! Now, sit down and tell me what's got you so all fired up."

"It's m'niece, Shelley, she's gone missing again, and I aim to punish the one that took her. This is the second time it's happened in this town, Chief. Can you clean up this crime spree or do I have to sue you?"

"Easy, Hortense. Tell me what happened."

"It's Shelley. She's gone. That's what happened. Last time I spoke to her, she was heading over to the Thomas's, something about joining in the treasure hunt. Flapdoodle, that's what it is. Flapdoodle. Ain't no treasure around here; just one of Steve's schemes. I never could understand what Suzanne saw in that man, a complete stranger yet."

"He's been here almost fifteen years, Hortense, and it was actually Skank Peterson who found the treasure map."

"Hmmph. That no account."

Nathan began writing. "So, when was it you saw your niece last?"

"About 7:00 this morning, heading over to the Thomas

44

place. And here it is 4:00 and nary a word from her. She told me she'd be home by lunch."

"Hmmm, Wanda was just in, telling me Phil hadn't made it home either. There may be something to this, Hortense. I'll look into it. Maybe that bunch just got caught up in their hunt for treasure," he chuckled.

"Well, she ain't answered her cellphone, if it means anythin' to you. I'll go," she said, picking up her gun, "but I want some action on this chief. You hear me?" She left the police station, firing at a squirrel as she did so.

Nathan picked up the papers on his desk and read thru them again, then asked Genevieve to get him Wanda Hawks at her Bed and Breakfast.

***

The group inside the tunnel was becoming uncomfortable. The air was stale and not moving at all, making for hot quarters. Pastor Kapas dabbed at his face. a hopeless look on him.

"Do you think your secretary might be looking for you Rev'ren?" Phil asked him.

"On vacation, she left town to go see her folks up in Hickory." He mopped some more.

"Rainey?" Steve asked.

"Skank left early this morning on a charter. He won't be back until nightfall and I gave Sharon the day off. Nothing happening at work."

"Brandan?"

"Emily knows I'm with you, she's handling the bicycle rental today. One of Kevin's girls is in the shop."

Nodding, he moved on to Bullet Head. who had joined the group that morning. "Nope, nobody knows I'm here. My lady, Genevieve? I haven't been in touch with her for an entire day. Far as I know she thinks I'm at the coffee bar."

Suzanne spoke up, "My coffee bar, who's manning it?"

"Probably one of the McLaughlin kids," Brandan offered.

Rainey put her head in her hands and wept. "We are so screwed!"

"Well, surely someone will see Large Bear's truck, or miss the pastor!"

"Don't count on it," Bullet Head told the group, "I could've sworn I heard it being driven away."

Rainey cried harder and louder. "For Pete's sake, Rainey, save your strength. Crying won't help," Suzanne admonished her.

Finally, Shelley spoke up. "Aunt Hortense knows where I went, and when. She'll do something, I'm sure."

"Yeah, shoot the chief," Steve chuckled, but admitted that it might be a good thing that Hortense knew about it all.

Suzanne cleared her throat, "Mrs. Happy Joe?" She looked at Large Bear.

"I'm on patrol tonight, I told her I was going there from our hunt. She won't look for me before morning, I'm afraid."

"So," Steve began, "We have to rely on either Hortense or the pastor's wife to sound the alarm. Let's just sit here and wait and see who comes to our rescue. Large Bear, you and Pastor better douse those lights and save the batteries. Besides, it will be cooler with them turned off anyway.

"I'm hungry", Rainey cried

***

After checking with Wanda, Nathan had the idea the group were headed to Pyke's Bay, but from there, she had no idea. Emily was too nervous waiting on word from Brandan. She closed the antique store, coffee bar, and bicycle shop, and headed up the hill to the Hawks Nest, where she waited on word with her mother-in-law.

Mrs. Kapas was not overly worried about her husband. He

was frequently called away. She had no idea he was with the treasure hunt folks.

It was Hortense, and the Hawks family who stewed over the situation. As twilight turned to darkness, their anxiety increased.

Skank decided to build a fire and stay on the island for the night. He dropped his charter off in Pykes Bay and headed out. Phoning home, he left a message on the answering machine for his wife, telling her he'd see her in the morning.

When Large Bear did not show up for his patrol, Nathan drove over to Pykes Bay to look around for any clue that his people had been there. He drove past a grove of trees where Large Bear's truck had been hidden, but he never saw it, and kept on driving.

In the tunnel the group huddled together for comfort, eventually falling asleep on the dank ground, it would be a long night for everyone.

Around midnight, Suzanne woke up with a start. Nudging Steve awake, she whispered that she was concerned for the "guys," Elvis and Dawg. Rainey had taken them to her house. Now, she was here, and Skank was out night fishing with his charter. She sidled over to Rainey and woke her up.

"Elvis and Dawg," she hissed. "Are they okay?"

Rainey yawned, nodded yes, and said Skank would take care of them, and went back to sleep.

Chapter Fourteen

Large Bear was instantly awake, his senses on full alert. He was sure he heard a truck up above them. Stealthily, he moved over to the entrance and listened, the noise getting louder. Yes, it was definitely a large vehicle, a truck hopefully.

He heard what sounded like a heavy pair of metal clippers, and suddenly, the opening was there, fresh air poured into the tunnel, and Nathan Sowinski, a spotlight in his hand was looking around at the astonished group.

"Everyone okay down there?" he shouted.

The treasure hunters were ecstatic to see him, waking up, smiling, and laughing at him. So happy to see a friendly face, the women wept tears of joy, and the men began helping the ladies to the outside. Everyone talked at once, asking how he found them, had he caught Farnsworth—or Mitchell—yet, and what time was it?

Checking out the group, Nathan decided they were unhurt, and in pretty good shape, except for being hungry, as Rainey loudly proclaimed.

"Okay, settle down now, people. Mrs. Happy Joe, Wanda, Hortense, and Mrs. Kapas are all waiting at the station for you. So, come on and we'll get you folks home."

"Skank?" Rainey asked

"Out on the island for the night. He said he'd see you in the morning." Nathan gave her an apologetic smile.

"That rat. I'll kill him," Rainey screamed, as she continued to harangue about her husband all the while Nathan was trying to get her in the police cruiser.

Telling her best friend that they'd pick up the animals in the morning, Steve said they'd walk home. They needed the fresh air. Large Bear was told his wife would take him to where he found his truck.

Goodnights were said all around and, as the Thomases began their walk home, they could still hear Lorraine hollering about Skank not being at home to welcome her.

Nathan's last words to them were to come by his office at 9:00 in the morning and he'd lay it all out for them. He tipped his cap to them as he drove away.

Chapter Fifteen

Emily Hawks had children she could not leave, but she happily welcomed Brandan home. Lorraine Brackett, Beryl's Cove's premier real estate agent, continued to rail against Skank all night. She found it hard to sleep when she was so angry and even threw a few things at the front door, scaring her Elsie as well as and Dawg and Elvis, who would not be picked up for several hours yet.

"Sorry guys", she murmured, as she tried once again to sleep.

Steve felt that after a hot shower, he and Suzanne would be in the mood for romance, He approached her, put his arms around her and nibbled on her ear.

She turned to face him, her hair still damp, and patted his cheek. "You go on to bed, I'm going to practice my violin a while."

Steve looked at her incredulously. "Now? It's nearly 1 a.m. Why not come to bed, for heaven's sake?"

"I know." she gently pushed him towards the staircase. "But I'm a little wired and this will relax me."

"So will making mad, passionate love to your adoring husband," Steve shouted from the landing. He knew that his wife released tension in different ways, but he couldn't justify practicing the violin at 1 in the morning.

As the screeching and scratching of the instrument drifted up to their bedroom, he put a pillow over his ears and finally drifted off to sleep. An hour later, Suzanne found him that way, removed the pillow from his head, kissed his cheek, and went to sleep herself. She told herself she'd make it up to him when they woke up, and she did.

***

Eight o'clock sharp in the morning, Steve was at Rainey's door to retrieve his animals. Dawg was delighted to see him, wagging his stump of a tail and slobbering all over the man. Elvis was his usual, aloof self and Steve laughed, knowing the cat would think up some horrible punishment for them. He put Dawg on his leash and carried Elvis the two blocks to their house, Elvis riding high on his shoulder, looking around as if he were king of the world, which, of course he considered himself to be.

Purrs and happy yelps greeted Suanne as she cuddled the animals at the homecoming. "Everything go okay?" she asked.

Running his hand through the silver hair that his wife loved so much, he grinned sheepishly at her. "It seems Rainey left the guys with Sharon, her secretary, then gave her the day off. The three of them—Elsie was the ringleader, I understand—got into the bags of pet food stored there and scattered it about quite nicely. No one to walk them, so they messed the floor by the back door and drank from the toilet. She realized the situation about 3 this morning, and went and got the pets and took them inside to the house. Quite a mess she has to face this morning and she's still hollering about Skank not being there to greet her last night. I don't want to be in his shoes when he gets home. Honestly, I don't."

Suzanne was trying hard not to laugh, but failed miserably. The two of them giggled all through breakfast. Unable to take Dawg to the coffee shop before going to Nathan's office, Steve promised the bulldog he'd take him as soon as they got home.

At 8:45, they set out to walk to the police station, arriving on the dot of 9 a.m. By 15 after, everyone was assembled in the office, Genevieve having distributed coffee to them all.

Nathan sat behind his big desk, and shuffled a few papers before he began. "First off," he began, "I'm happy you all were unhurt, and I could get to you before the oxygen ran out."

Hortense was not to be mollified. She sat glaring at the police chief, her gun on the floor beside her.

The chief took a moment to clear his throat and began again. "I found Large Bear's truck as I was turning around and starting back from Pyke's Bay. I trust it was in good order." He looked at the Indian, who nodded.

"I recognized it as Large Bear's, and checked it out. I saw that the mag lite he always carried in the back was missing. Now where, I asked myself, would he need a mag lite, I wondered. The logical answer, of course, was someplace dark and dreary." The chief was trying to keep the amusement from his voice, but he found it a little more than ludicrous that this group of so-called adults had been chasing after some hidden treasure. He cleared his throat once more.

"Okay, I hope you 'kids' had a good adventure, but I want to get serious now." He picked up a paper that had come in just that morning from the FBI. "Old man Phillips—his name was Martin—he had a daughter somewhere along the line. Never married the mother, and she and the kid split before the girl learned to walk. That's when Phillips took to being a semi-recluse and doing shine. The locals, like Suzanne's father, knew him and so did the Feds. They were after him all the time. Never could catch the wily old goat or find his still. Anyway, this daughter grew up, married a man named Harley Mitchell, and had a son, Garrett. Garrett Mitchell is our perp, the guy who locked you in the tunnel. A real no-account, from what I understand a flim-flam artist of the nth degree. Poses as all sorts of characters, and this Trilby guy was just a hanger on type of person. Apparently, Mitchell got tired of him hangin' around, and I think killed him, although we have no forensic evidence of that just yet."

"Was he the one who sent us on a wild goose chase, Chief, and why?"

"I'm gettin to that Rainey. To answer your question, yes. He was. The Feds think Phillips' girlfriend stuck around long enough to figure out he was moonshining and making fistfuls of money from it. She wanted it, told the daughter and grandson about it, and lay-about Mitchell decided to go after it. I'm guessing the grandmother figured out where it was buried, but Mitchell wanted someone else to do his digging for him. Thus, the planted clues, hoping someone would find them, go to the buried treasure—whatever it was—and dig it up for him. You did, too.

Mrs. Happy Joe was thoroughly disgusted, shook her head, and gave Large Bear an unhappy face.

Nathan continued, "Did you find anything down in that tunnel?"

Shelley spoke up, "yes, we did, Chief, but this Mitchell guy evidently followed us, took the strongbox from us, and locked us in." She smiled at her aunt, "Quite an adventure for an out of towner, I'd say."

Nathan watched in horror as Hortense stood up and aimed her gun at him again. "Now Hortense, I told you before, don't be aimin' that thing at me, or I'll have you locked up, and I mean it!"

Hortense put her gun down, and glared at the chief. "What you aimin' to do 'bout this, Chief. M'niece and all these folks coulda been killed while you sit there laughin' at 'em!"

Nathan put up his splayed hands in front of the group. "Aw right, folks, settle down. I have an APB out for Mitchell. We'll get him. Eventually. When we do, he'll be charged with kidnapping, littering, or anything else I can throw at him. In the meantime, the government lab boys are trying to find something, *anything*, that will lead to Mitchell as the murderer of Trilby. That's all I know. That's all I can tell you, besides the fact that I am truly happy none of you were hurt during this escapade.

"Now, on a lighter note, the Yacht club is having their

midsummer dance Saturday night. My brother Paul and his group are playing. I would love to see ya'll there. We need a little lightness after all this, don't you think?"

Nods and assents all around, as the group left the office. Pastor Kapas hung back a little and grinned at Nathan. "I smell a sermon in all this, don't you Chief?"

Laughing, Nathan grinned at him and waved him on. When everyone had left, he spun around in his chair and watched as they all headed for their respective homes, a big smile on his face.

Chapter Sixteen

The man sat on the edge of his bed, rubbing the stubble on his face. He looked at the lock box on the motel dresser and felt disgust. The lock on the small, metal box was a combination lock, and Mitchell had no way of knowing how to get into it. If he shot the lock, the noise would bring someone around. If he hammered it, that noise too would bring someone.

He had driven away from the Tri-Bay area soon after he locked those locals in the tunnel. He was now in New Bern, where his aged mother lived. He'd told her he'd bring whatever treasure he found. Now, he couldn't even get to the stuff inside and knew he could not call a local locksmith, which would raise suspicion. His mother didn't know he was back because he had stopped at a local motel just outside of town when he left the coast.

What did she know or care, anyway. The hell with it, he thought, the hell with her. What was in the box was going to make him rich. He didn't need her or anyone, ever again. Pulling on his shoes, he left the room securing the lock box under the front seat of his battered truck. He cursed himself for not taking the nice pickup that was parked outside the tunnel, leaving it abandoned instead. It sure made his old heap of a truck look worse.

He peeled out of the parking space, throwing dust and pebbles in his wake, and headed for the highway. He had to get away, someplace where there would be a locksmith, and he'd get this sucker opened once and for all. He knew it was just loaded with his grandfather's shine money. He could feel the wad of bills in his pocket already.

The desk clerk at the motel Mitchell had just left, was

going through the morning mail, when he came across a flyer from the FBI. Reading it, he realized it was an all-points bulletin on the FBI's latest fugitive list. He stared at the face of Mitchell, the man in room 34.

"Oh my God," he shouted, and ran from the office down to room 34. The man was gone, not a thing left inside the room. He had run off without paying the bill too. Going as fast as he could, he reentered the office and reached for the phone, dialing the operator.

"Gimme the FBI" he shouted..

***

Late Saturday afternoon, the town of Beryl's Cove was preparing for their annual mid-summer dance. Flowers were being delivered to the yacht club, container trucks were unloading pallets of food at the club's kitchen door, and the wait staffers were all busy turning the dining room into a ballroom.

Nathan's brother, Paul, led a band from Raleigh. They were setting up a bandstand at one end of the room. They carried a portable stage with them and were securing it in place. Several of the musicians were tuning their instruments, and Paul's brother had shown up to welcome them back to town. They talked softly in a corner.

Around five, some of the townspeople began showing up for an early dinner before the dance started at 7. Emily and Brandan had asked one of the McLaughlin's teenagers to babysit and were enjoying cocktails on the wraparound porch, as they waited on Wanda and Phil to show up.

Pastor Kapas and his wife always enjoyed these dances and sat sipping glasses of wine, while they waited on their meal.

All four of the Hawkses were enjoying a steak dinner when Rainey and Skank came in. Rainey looked beautiful in a

Royal Blue, off the shoulder, tea-length dress, a sparkling necklace of gorgeous sapphires at her throat.

Wanda nudged her daughter-in-law to notice the necklace. Leaning towards Emily, she hissed in her ear, "Every time she and Skank have a falling out, she gets another piece of jewelry. Pretty soon she'll have a collection worthy of the crown jewels." Both women laughed, and watched as Skank, looking positively gentlemanly, held the chair for his wife to sit down.

Part of the fun of these dances, was seeing the locals come out in their finery. Most of them were hardworking shop owners, dressed in work clothes during the day, and they reveled in being able to dress up and let their hair down at these functions.

Mrs. Happy Joe always wore some sort of brightly colored outfit, turquoise bangles at her wrist, and always with a pretty feather in her hair. Large Bear, who everyone knew was the world's largest human being, was striking in his dark trousers and white shirt, a bolo tie hanging from his collar.

At 6:30, Steve and Suzanne walked out their back door, across the yard to the club parking lot, and entered the yacht club. Steve in a dark suit and Suzanne in a strawberry-colored short cocktail dress, they were a stunning-looking couple and heads did turn when they entered the room. Rainey raised her hand and motioned them to the two chairs they had saved for them. The four of them had no sooner ordered their meal than the dancing began.

Whirling his beautiful wife around the dance floor always made Steve feel like a million dollars. He mused often about the circumstances surrounding his meeting Suzanne. So lucky he was, and Suzanne would probably agree with him; he chuckled to himself over that thought. As annoying as Lorraine could be, he would always be grateful to her for sending him towards Coldwell antiques that day. Putting up with his wife's best friend, he tried to remember that.

At some point during the evening, Steve and Nathan met up at the bar. "What's the latest on Mitchell?" Steve asked, while he waited on their drinks to be ready.

"FBI says he was spotted at a motel in New Bern but left in a hurry. They've tracked him as far in the state as Pinehurst, to an old, rundown mansion on the edge of the golf course there. As I understand it, they are waiting for confirmation that it's really him. Then I reckon they'll go in after him."

Steve accepted the two drinks and turned to ask the chief one more question, before returning to Suzanne and the others at their table. "Any sign of a metal box with him?" They had no sooner returned to the dinner table together than Bullet Head breezed by, Genevieve on his arm.

"Hey, Swabby," he cackled, "found any more tunnels we could get locked into?" Laughing, he moved away, swaying to the music with Genevieve."

"Trilbys' death, Nathan, Mitchell do it?'

"FED boys told me there was some DNA evidence to that effect, and I'm sure it will all come out at trial. Right now they have him on kidnapping charges and grand theft auto only, but the investigation is hardly over. I'll let you know."

It was then that Paul's band segued into a swing number and Steve sat pensively, watching all the dancers on the dance floor.

"What is it?" His wife asked him.

"The treasure. It's still out there."

"Oh Steve, drop it. What could possibly be in that lock box that is so important?"

"Curiosity, Suze honey, it's really got me now. You just never know what might be in that box. Want to go find out?"

"All the way to Pinehurst?"

"Sure, once on the mainland it's not so awfully far, we leave early enough, we can get there by noon."

Chapter Seventeen

Hearing from Phil about Steve wanting to travel to Pinehurst, Nathan showed up at the Thomas home at 7:30 the next morning, just as Steve and Suzanne, Rainey and Phil were getting into the car. Pastor Kapas, casting a sidelong look at his wife, decided he had had enough adventure. Brandan said he couldn't leave the bike shop any longer and Shelley went back home, at the urging. of her Aunt Hortense. Bullet Head absolutely had to get back to work. So, it was just the four of them again. At the last moment, Large Bear showed up in his truck, prepared to follow. At the same time, the police chief had walked up to the driver's side window to speak to Steve.

"Forget it," he began. "Feds got him last night and took him into custody."

"The lockbox?" Phil asked.

"I told the feds that Phillips' kin lived in these parts and were entitled to whatever was in the box. He turned to leave, but remembered something. "The lock box is being Fed Exed to me today, and before we turn it over to some distant cousins, or Mitchell's mother, you can come by the office and see what you missed." He tipped his hat to the group and walked away laughing.

Later that afternoon, the treasure hunters, without Shelley, gathered in the chief's office to open the box. Nathan had hired a locksmith from Baylor's Point to come by and release the lock on it. They all stood in a circle around the chief's desk as he gingerly opened it.

Pushing his hat to the top of his head, he stood with hands on hips, looking inside, "Well, I'll be", he said while he turned the box to face his visitors. "Confederate money."

"What? All this time we've been chasing worthless Confederate money?"

"Looks that way," He moved the banded stack of bills aside and lifted a piece of paper out of the lockbox. "Here, what's this?" Unfolding the paper, Nathan saw that it was a deed of some kind. "This is a deed to that worthless cabin, Steve, that you and Suzanne ran up on that day. Here's another envelope."

Opening it, he counted out $200 in small bills, and laid all of it out on his desk. Grinning at the group, he sat back down again. "So, it looks like you were chasing $200 that rightfully goes to Mitchell's mother, some worthless piece of property, and Confederate money." He couldn't help the laughter that came out. "You guys sure got yourselves into a mess of trouble over all this, I hope you learned your lesson."

At the thought of Beryl's Coves leading citizens chasing all over the coast for a non-existent treasure was just too much, the group left the police station, Nathan's laughter echoing in their ears. As they stood outside the building, looking shamefully at one another, Large Bear looked at the group before him.

"I'm goin' home. Don't get me involved in any more schemes this summer!" he said and drove off.

Phil looked at Steve. "What are you guys doing now?"

Suzanne took her husband's arm and started walking towards Eventide Lane and their home. "We're going up to the mountain house for at least a month! See you when we get back!"

Chapter Eighteen

After an eight-hour drive, the Thomas couple arrived at their mountain home in Ridgeville. They paid a caretaker to tend to the place over the winter and spring and found that all was in order. Stopping at the small general store in town, they picked up some fresh produce and steaks for dinner, as well as some dog and cat treats for the pets.

Pulling into the driveway, Steve made note that the lawn had been freshly mowed. The Koi pond he had put in last year was clean and the fish appeared to be thriving. Elvis's favorite pastime had always been watching the fish swim around in it.

Once inside, Suzanne put the groceries away, while Steve checked out the air conditioning and the plumbing. Elvis and Dawg zoomed around the place, checking under beds and sniffing what seemed every square inch of the house. Assured that all was well, they flopped down in front of the French doors that led from the great room onto the patio. Asleep in minutes, they snored happily while Suzanne prepared supper and Steve went out to the garage and plugged in his golf cart. He wanted a full charge in the morning when he went into town.

Around 9 that night, a loud knock at the door startled all of them. Dawg went to the door to greet whoever was there. Steve opened it to see his best friend, Gregg standing there. They greeted each other warmly and Gregg moved inside to buss Suzanne on the cheek.

"Sit down, sit down. How'd you know we were here? I was going to go up to the Inn tomorrow morning and check out if you and Bev were here."

"We pulled in about a week ago. Glad you're here. We

saw the car drive past, heading this way." He stopped long enough to pat the animals on their heads. Dawg moved his massive head onto Gregg's lap, with a healthy slobber.

"Fishing at dawn in the morning. Roscoe's going along and Jean said come to supper tomorrow night. We'll eat what we catch. Gotta run." With that, he pulled his hefty self off the couch, and walked to the door with a wave, leaving Steve and Suzanne in giggles.

"The guy never changes— a laugh a minute." Once the front door shut, Steve wrapped his arms around his wife and nuzzled her neck. "What say we make it an early night, gorgeous?"

"Aha, getting frisky, are we?"

As they walked arm in arm down the hall Dawg and Elvis fell asleep to the sound of their laughter.

***

Dawn brought Steve up to the back door of the Nest O' Rest Inn that Gregg's sister and brother-in-law owned and operated. Dawg was with him, anxious to get started.

Roscoe came out first, followed in a few minutes by Gregg, loaded down with fishing gear, a donut in his free hand. Steve grabbed the pastry out of his hand, fed it to Dawg, and admonished his buddy for eating junk like that, especially since he had diabetes.

"Here, Have some grapes, they're better for you."

"Yeah, but they look so disgustingly healthy."

Roscoe laughed at their antics and led the way to the river that meandered through his property. In no time at all, the three men were casting lines and sitting on folding stools, swapping lies and stories to one another while Dawg chased bugs and lizards that had come out to sun themselves.

Steve couldn't resist the opportunity to regale his friends with the story of his treasure hunt, plus the dead body—

possibly murdered—that had been found after the hurricane swamped the huge gulley behind the Hawks Nest B-and-B. The men were amazed, and visibly impressed with all the goings on in Beryl's Cove.

"Unbelievable", they said, in unison.

***

The parking area of the Nest O' Rest Inn was full. Jean had a full house of guests. Once they had eaten breakfast and dispersed for the day, she rode off with Suzanne for some girl talk and shopping. Hungrier than she thought she'd be at lunchtime, Jean suggested they pull into a little tearoom tucked behind the hardware store.

The alley that led to the tearoom was paved with bricks, and hanging baskets of flowers, and large, potted plants lined the walk to the tearoom, which was called, Gracie's Place.

"Is this restaurant new, Jean?" Suzanne inquired as they found a table by a picture window that looked out on a pretty greenway behind all the shops.

"Been here a few years, but you gotta look for it. I don't think Gracie advertises. She doesn't need to, really. It's always full when I come here."

After ordering glasses of iced tea, and sandwiches, the women caught each other up on their current activities. Jean, too, was astounded by the treasure hunt and goings on in the Cove.

"Isn't that just like a man?", she laughed, "always chasing something they can't have."

Over a delicious Flan with butterscotch sauce, they ordered coffee to finish off the meal.

"Jean, I don't think I ever heard the story of how you and Roscoe met and came up here. You're not originally a Carolina girl are you?"

"Uh uh, no. Gregg and I were born in Chicago. When

Gregg went off to the Navy, I went away to college."

"Oh? what school?"

"Oh, it was a little place called Normal, Illinois. They have a teachers' college there, or did at the time. Although I'm thinking now it's just a regular school, but at the time, it trained teachers. Kinda like Appalachian State here, which used to be called a teacher's college. Anyway, I met Roscoe, and we both harbored a secret desire to being innkeepers. He worked in business for a while, while we saved up enough money to buy something, and I scoured the country for just the right place. Ridgeville appealed to us both. We built the inn, you know."

Finishing her coffee, Suzanne put down her cup. "No, I wasn't aware you built it. You certainly did a fine job. I love the inn. It's beautiful and in a wonderful setting. I know Gregg and Bev love it up here, as do we." She smiled.

"Oh, don't get me started on my brother. He's always been a scamp of the first order. The trouble he got us into as kids, it's unbelievable we lived through our childhood. He did tell me about you and Steve meeting in your antique store, and it went from there."

Suzanne laughed, "Boy, did it ever. I didn't even like him when we first met, nor did I trust him—him and his Elvis memorabilia. I thought it was a joke."

"Oh, I can imagine. How's his shop doing anyway? Norfolk is it?"

"Yes, it's doing well, but his assistant, MJ, is wanting to retire. So Steve is thinking of selling it. It's a lot of trouble and we're getting older. You know how that goes."

With a nod from Jean, the two left the tearoom to continue with their shopping, hoping the men were catching dinner for them.

Chapter Nineteen

The three of them sat on their stools, totally dejected. It was 4 in the afternoon and they had not even had a nibble. Gregg was beside himself, his reputation as an expert fisherman was on the line. He, most of all, should have caught a trout or *something.*

"What're we gonna do?" Steve asked.

Roscoe shrugged, and Gregg had a strange look on his face.

"Let's go into town and buy the fish. The girls will never know the difference and we can walk in with our heads held high."

Gregg's cackle filled the air as they all piled into the golf cart. Gregg was in front with Steve. Roscoe sat in the back seat, his arm around Dawg, as they sped off into town. The golf cart could be seen all over town, zipping into first one store and then then another, looking for fresh fish. Everything was prepackaged, which did not suit Gregg at all. He wanted whole, fresh fish, two or three of them.

It was much later, and the three of them still zoomed on the golf cart, Dawgs stump tail working furiously. He was thoroughly enjoying the ride.

Back at the inn, Suzanne was getting worried. She had gone home to check on Elvis and change clothes before returning to Jean's place. Still, no sign of the men. "Aren't you worried, Jean?"

"Nope. Evidently they didn't catch anything. So they have gone in search of our dinner. Knowing Gregg, he'll come in with some fish, claim they had a grand time catching them, and he'll think I believe him."

"He's pulled this before," Bev added. She had come in

from the patio, opting not to go to town earlier. She stayed behind to sunbathe and rest and just now entered the dining room to help set the table.

Hands on her hips, Jean. looked over at the table, satisfied that it was ready. She suggested they go into the great room and have a glass of wine while they waited on the men. "I've got it covered, girls. There is a fresh fish market out on the highway and Gregg usually goes there, when all else fails, to buy the fish. I've already called and told them to be on the lookout for them. They should be back soon," she said, as she settled into a comfortable chair.

The three of them laughed as they thought about the men zooming around in Steve's golf cart.

They didn't have to wait long. Steve pulled up to the back door and they brought three big fish inside, grinning from ear to ear.

Jean, Bev, and Suzanne laughed as they took the fish from Gregg and shooed them out of the kitchen.

"Dinner in forty-five minutes," Jean giggled as she shut the door on them.

The men each enjoyed a beer in the great room, as they wondered what was so funny.

***

It was later that night, after they were home, that Steve and Suzanne sat on their patio enjoying the cooler night and star gazing. Steve reached for his wife's hand.

"Tell me, Mrs. Thomas, are you a happy woman?"

"Mmmnn, let me see. Are you going to be chasing any more treasures, Mr. Thomas?"

Steve shook his head, as he kissed her hand. "Nope."

"Solve any more crimes?"

He went up her arm, kissing it while he did so. "Don't plan on it," he murmured.

"Chase after other women?" she teased.

"Definitely not," he replied, while kissing her lips.

"Then, I am most definitely a happy woman Mr. Thomas." She flashed her most brilliant smile at him, as he helped her out of the chair.

Once inside, they locked the patio door behind them and turned out the lights.

PART 2

The Nest O' Rest Inn*

Sitting in the High Country of the North Carolina Mountains, this Inn is noted for hospitality and good food. AND, when Gregg and Bev Powell are there, fine entertainment.

Jean used to have a 5-star chef but, temperamental as he was, he walked out one day. So Jean does the cooking now. Here, she shares just a few of her specialties with you.

All recipes are for 4 people but can be doubled to accommodate more guests.

Frozen Fruit Salad
- 1 reg. sized can of fruit salad
- 1 pkg cream cheese
- 1 container of whipped cream
- 3/4 to 1 cup mayonnaise
- Jar of maraschino cherries

Combine softened cream cheese, whipped cream and mayonnaise (amount to taste) in square pan. Add drained fruit salad and 1/2 the jar of cut up cherries. Add some of the cherry juice to the mixture for color and smooth it all out. Place and store in freezer. Salad should be ready when solid—about 4 hours

Salmon Casserole
- 1 large can of salmon
- minced dry onions
- soda crackers
- white sauce

Drain and cull the salmon, add a tablespoon of dry, minced onions. and crumbled up soda crackers (12 to 15). Mix well, and pour white sauce over the mix (milk butter, and enough flour to thicken it). Place sliced cheddar cheese across the top of the casserole, and bake on 350° for 35 minutes.

Cheese Biscuits

Use a good 4 cups Jiffy Baking mix—add milk until mixture is "pliable." Add heaping cup of shredded cheddar cheese (coarse ground is best), mix well with hands, and put on floured board to knead. Do not overwork the dough. Cut out biscuits and place on greased cookie sheet, baking at 375° for 12 minutes or so, depending on your oven. Serve with country ham.

Pork Chop Casserole

Brown well 4 boneless pork chops and cut up into bite sided pieces and place in casserole dish. Melt 2 pkgs of Colby Jack cheese with 2 cans of cream of mushroom soup. Peel and slice 2 baking potatoes and add to the cut up porkchops. THEN add the melted cheese/soup mixture before baking it. When the soup/cheese mixture is melted, pour over the pork chops, and bake 2 1/2 hours on 325° (to avoid burning the cheese, cover with foil for the first hour, remove foil, and continue baking for another hour).

Asparagus Souffle

- 1 can of asparagus spears
- milk
- 4 eggs

•shredded cheddar cheese

Drain asparagus juice into measuring cup, add enough milk to equal 2 cups of liquid—set aside. Separate the eggs, beating the whites into a fluffy meringue—set aside. Add 2 cups of the shredded cheddar to the egg yolks and set aside. Take the asparagus juice/milk mixture and heat on stove, adding 3 tab. butter and 5 tab. flour until it is thickened into a sauce. Salt and pepper to, taste. Add the egg yolk/ cheese mixture until thoroughly blended. Pour in the drained asparagus, and finally, fold in the egg whites. Set casserole dish inside another dish filled with water, and bake 1 hour on 400"

* Remember, this is a work of fiction, the recipes are those of the author, but if there really was a Nest O" Rest Inn they would be a smash sensation!

PART 3

A Final Word from Dawg and Elvis

Lying in their favorite sunbeam, whether at the coast or in the mountains, Dawg and Elvis frequently converse with one another. So long as no humans are around, of course.

Elvis was stretched out his full length on the little rug that Mama Suzanne provides for him at the patio door. No bare floor for THIS cat, he deserves only the best. Dawg, being of the slobbering kind, can park his ample butt on the floor.

"So, what d'ya think, Dawg?"

The bulldog rolled over on his side and cast a glance at the cat. "Bout what?" he yawned.

"You know, this treasure hunt business Dad was on. Typical human behavior, if you ask me. Like dogs, chasing their tail." Elvis sat up and stared at his canine companion.

"I haven't got a tail', Dawg replied, as he rolled over on his other side.

"I know that, dummy, but if you did, believe me, you'd be chasing it." Elvis sat up and chattered at a squirrel that was on the patio. He lunged at it, but hit the door instead.

Dawg rolled on his back laughing, "Now, who's a dummy," he chuckled, "at least I don't bang into doors!" It was all too funny for Dawg, as he rolled around, scratching his back. "Dummy, dummy, dummy."

"Hush up, you mangy beast, I'm the king around here."

Dawg sat up suddenly and watched as Steve approached the two of them. "Here comes Dad, I'll bet he's gonna take me somewhere, while you lay here in your sunbeam, na, na, na, noo, noo."

He wiggled his stump tail, while Elvis, observing this ridiculous display of pandering to humans, rolled over on his side again. Facing the door, he sighed. "It's all so tedious, this

73

raising of humans."
   He was asleep in seconds.